# The Happy Prince and The Selfish Giant

Nelson

**Thomas Nelson and Sons Ltd**
Nelson House  Mayfield Road
Walton-on-Thames  Surrey
KT12 5PL  UK

**Nelson Blackie**
Wester Cleddens Road
Bishopbriggs
Glasgow  G64 2NZ  UK

**Thomas Nelson Australia**
102 Dodds Street
South Melbourne
Victoria 3205  Australia

**Nelson Canada**
1120 Birchmount Road
Scarborough  Ontario
M1K 5G4  Canada

© Thomas Nelson and Sons Ltd 1991
'The Happy Prince' by Oscar Wilde was adapted by Ron Deadman and illustrated
by Anna Hancock
'The Selfish Giant' by Oscar Wilde was adapted by Ron Deadman and illustrated
by Derek Collard

First published by Macmillan Education Ltd 1987

This edition published by Thomas Nelson and Sons Ltd 1992

I(T)P   Thomas Nelson is an International
          Thomson Publishing Company

I(T)P   is used under licence

ISBN 0-17-422527-X
NPN 9  8  7  6

Printed in China

# The Happy Prince

Once there was a Happy Prince.
He was a statue and stood on a column
high above his city. He was covered all over with
leaves of fine gold, and instead of eyes, he had two
bright jewels. On the handle of his sword there was
another jewel, a large red ruby.

Every day the people of the city came to look at
the Prince. They were very proud of him and knew
he would never leave them.

One day a little swallow flew over the city.
All his friends had gone away to a warmer,
sunnier land weeks before, but he had stayed behind
because he had loved the beautiful reeds on
the river bank. The other swallows had told him
he was foolish to stay, for winter was coming.

Soon the swallow found out they were right and
he began to shiver in the cold.

"Oh, how I wish I was in the land of the sun,"
he said. "I will go there tomorrow. But first
I must find some shelter for the night."

Suddenly he saw the statue on the tall column above the city.

"I will rest there," he said and closed his eyes. But then a drop of water fell on him.

"How strange!" said the swallow. "There isn't a cloud in the sky, yet it is raining."

He looked up and saw it wasn't raining. The drops of water were tears from the statue. The Prince was crying.

The swallow felt sorry for the Prince because
he looked so sad.

"Why are you crying?" he asked.

"Because I can see so much misery in the streets
below us in the city," said the Prince. "My people
are poor and hungry and I would like to help them,
but I can't move. You could help them, little bird.
You could make my people happy."

"How can I do that?" asked the swallow.

"Take the jewel from my sword," said the Prince.
"Take it to a poor woman whose little boy is
ill in bed."

"But I must fly to the land of the sun," said the swallow. "Soon the snow will come and cover us both with his cold blanket."

"Little swallow," said the Prince. "I beg you to help me. The little boy is crying for oranges, but his mother can give him nothing but water. Take the jewel. It will save the boy's life."

The swallow looked up at the Prince. "I will do as you ask," he said. "But tomorrow I must fly south and find the sun."

He took the jewel from the Prince's sword and
flew with it to the poor woman's house. He placed it
carefully on the table. Then he flew across to the
boy's bed and fanned him with his wings. The boy
smiled in his sleep, and the swallow knew that
his mother would be happy too when she found
the precious jewel. With it she could buy food and
drink and oranges for her child.

He flew back to the statue. "It is strange, Prince,
very strange. I feel quite warm now," he said.

"That is because you have helped somebody," said
the Prince. "Tomorrow you must do another good deed."

The next day the Prince said,
"There is a young man I can see.
He is trying to write a play, but he is cold and
hungry in his little room. You must help him."

"But I have taken the ruby from your sword,"
said the swallow.

"Now you must take one of my eyes," said the Prince.

The little bird shuddered. "I can't take one of
your eyes," he said. "That would be cruel."

"You must do as I say," said the Prince.

So the swallow took one of the Prince's eyes and flew down to the young writer, who was fast asleep in bed. Then, weeping at what he had done, he flew back to the Prince.

"Please good Prince," he said. "Let me go now to the land of the sun."

"Not yet, little swallow," said the Prince. "Listen carefully. You must now take the last jewel I have. You must take the bright jewel that is my other eye."

"I can't! I can't!" the swallow cried. "If I do that, you will be blind."

"Take the jewel and give it to a little girl who is selling matches," said the Prince. "She has dropped them in a puddle and her father will beat her if she goes home without any money."

The swallow wept in pity and horror as he obeyed the Prince. He found the little girl and placed the jewel gently in her hand. Then he flew back to his friend.

"I shall never leave you now, my Prince," he said. "How could I? You are now blind."

"Ah, little swallow, how good you are," said the
Prince. "You are my eyes now. Tomorrow you must
take a fine gold leaf from my body and give it to
the poorest person you can find in the city."

Sadly, and shivering in the cold wind, the swallow
obeyed. Every day he took the gold leaves off the
statue and gave them to the poorest people he could
find in the city.

They couldn't believe their eyes.

"Gold!" they cried. "This is wonderful! Now we can
buy food and milk for our children!" They laughed
with joy and sang in the streets.

But the swallow knew that he would never sing again. He would never see the land of the sun, or meet his friends again.

The snow came to the city, then the cruel frost. The swallow had just enough strength to fly up and perch on his friend's shoulder.

"Good Prince," he said. "Will you let me kiss you?"

"Yes, little swallow," said the Prince. "I know that you must go now and find the sun. Goodbye, dear friend."

"Ah no," said the swallow. "Good Prince, I am going to die." He kissed the Prince and then he fell dead at his feet.

At that moment a terrible cracking sound was heard all over the city. It was like ice cracking. It was like mountains falling apart.

The Prince's heart had broken with grief at the death of his little friend.

Early next morning the rich people of the city were walking in the square. They looked up at the statue and they were amazed.

"What has happened to his jewels and his fine gold leaves?" they said. "He looks dull and grey. We don't want an old statue like that."

So they pulled the statue down. They threw the broken heart of the statue on a dust heap outside the city walls.

And on this same dust heap lay the body of a little bird. The broken heart of a Prince who had once been happy, and the frozen body of a little swallow lay side by side in the dust.

Then something happened which the rich people of the city would never be able to understand.

God looked down on the city and sent for one of his angels.

"Go to the city," he said, "and bring me the most beautiful and the kindest things you can find."

The angel found the dust heap. He found the Prince's broken heart and the dead little bird.
He took them back to Heaven.

"You have chosen the finest things on Earth," God said. "You have chosen a kind heart and a faithful friend."

# The Selfish Giant

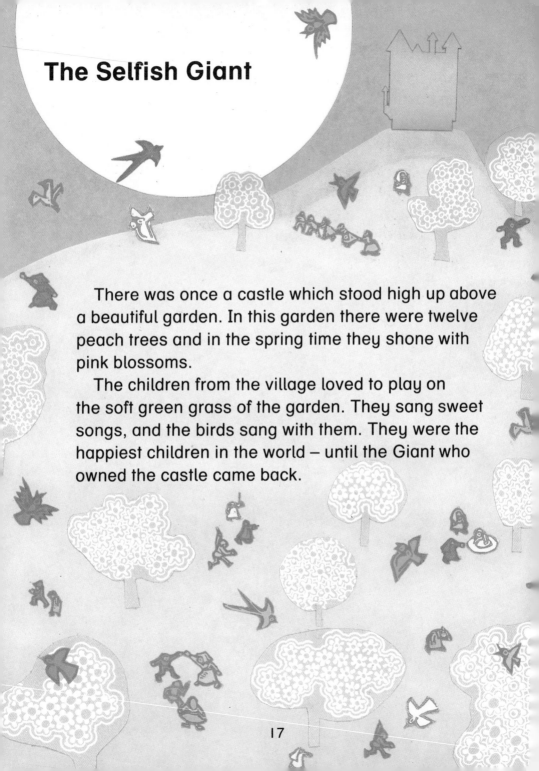

There was once a castle which stood high up above a beautiful garden. In this garden there were twelve peach trees and in the spring time they shone with pink blossoms.

The children from the village loved to play on the soft green grass of the garden. They sang sweet songs, and the birds sang with them. They were the happiest children in the world – until the Giant who owned the castle came back.

He was a huge, hairy Selfish Giant. He did not want
to share his garden with anyone. When he came home
from visiting his friend the Cornish Ogre, he heard
the children playing and the birds singing.

"What are you doing here?" he roared. "Clear off!"

He waved his huge arms around in rage and knocked
down one of the beautiful peach trees. The children
were so frightened they ran for their lives.

"They won't come here again," roared the Giant.
"I know how to keep them out."

He found bricks and stones and built a high wall round the garden. Then he found some wood and made a large notice board. On it he wrote these words:

KEEP OUT!

STAY AWAY FROM MY GARDEN!

Then he remembered the notice boards he had seen in Cornwall, so he put a second one up and on it he wrote these words:

TRESPASSERS WILL BE PROSECUTED!

"That will frighten them," he muttered. "That means they will be sent to prison if they come here again."

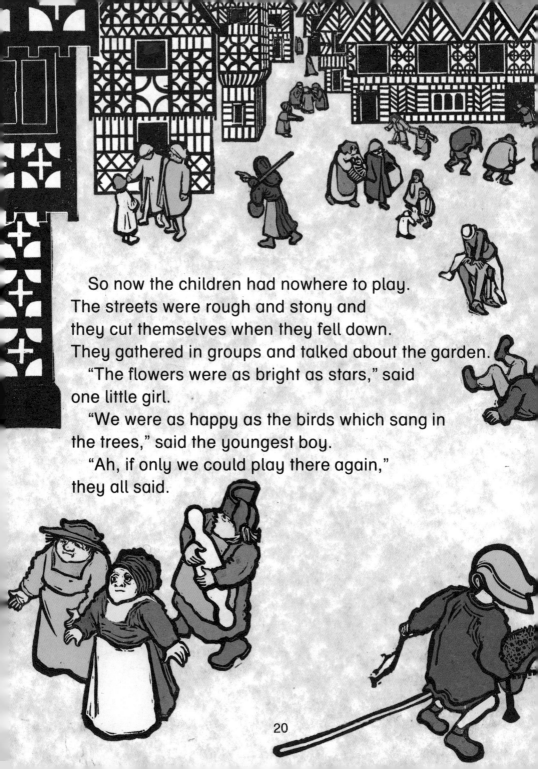

So now the children had nowhere to play.
The streets were rough and stony and
they cut themselves when they fell down.
They gathered in groups and talked about the garden.
   "The flowers were as bright as stars," said
one little girl.
   "We were as happy as the birds which sang in
the trees," said the youngest boy.
   "Ah, if only we could play there again,"
they all said.

Winter came and the snow piled high in the streets of the village and round the walls of the garden. The frost made patterns on the windows of the houses, and the children blew on their fingers to keep them warm.

Soon however spring came and the ice melted. The snow disappeared from all the gardens of the world. All except one.

In the garden of the Selfish Giant it was still winter. The spring did not like selfish people and stayed away from his garden.

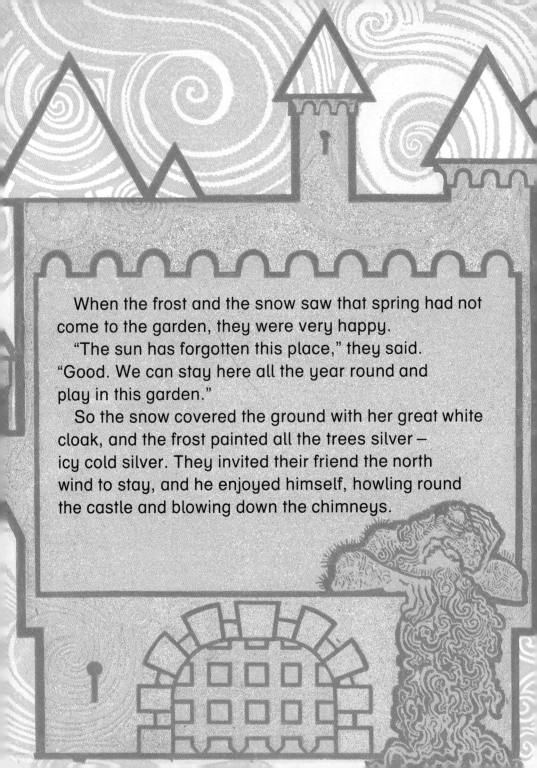

When the frost and the snow saw that spring had not come to the garden, they were very happy.

"The sun has forgotten this place," they said. "Good. We can stay here all the year round and play in this garden."

So the snow covered the ground with her great white cloak, and the frost painted all the trees silver — icy cold silver. They invited their friend the north wind to stay, and he enjoyed himself, howling round the castle and blowing down the chimneys.

The Selfish Giant sat in the window of the room which led out into his garden. He listened to the bitter north wind and the hailstones which the wind was throwing against the castle roof.

"I cannot understand it," the Giant said to himself, shivering and shaking his head. "When will the spring come and make the flowers grow again in my garden? I am tired of winter and want to sit outside in the sun."

But spring did not come to the garden that year. Nor did summer. Nor did autumn.

Golden fruits appeared on all the trees in the land, all except in the Giant's garden. There it was always winter. It was the coldest garden in the world.

But one day something strange happened. The Giant woke up one morning and began to groan with misery and shiver and shake with cold. Then he sat up straight in bed. He thought he could hear music coming from his garden. How strange!

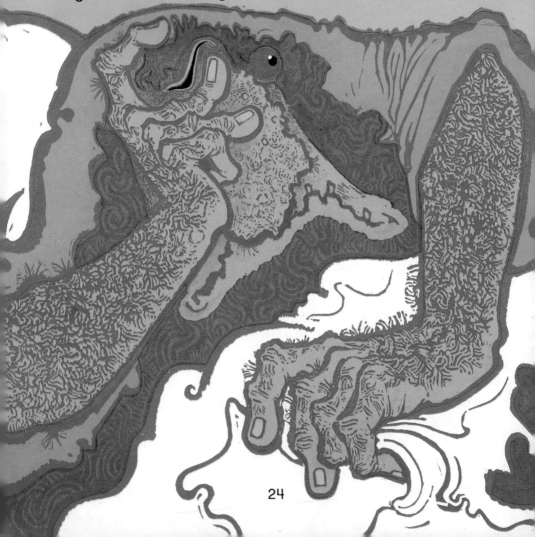

Music? Perhaps he was dreaming. He pinched himself hard, but no, he was awake, and he could hear music! Perhaps the King had sent his best fiddler to play for him to cheer him up.

Then suddenly he knew what the sound was. It was a bird – a little linnet. He had almost forgotten how beautiful birdsong could be. This was wonderful! But so strange!

And there was another mystery. The hail had stopped rattling on his roof, and the north wind was silent. Why was that?

He jumped out of bed and looked out of the window. Then he rubbed his eyes. Was his imagination playing him tricks? No. Some children had crept into the garden through a hole in the wall. They were sitting in the branches of the trees, and the trees were covered in pink blossoms.

"Spring has come at last!" cried the Giant. "At last!"

Then he looked down at the far corner of the garden. In this corner it was still winter.

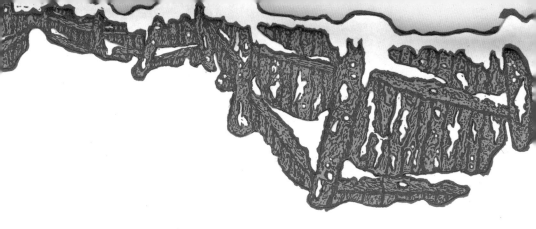

Why had spring forgotten one tiny corner of the garden? Suddenly the Giant knew why.

There was a little boy standing there. He was trying to reach up to the branches of a tree, but he was too small. He was crying and was very sad. The Giant ran out into the garden. He reached the spot where the little boy stood. Then he bent down and lifted him gently into the tree.

The children had run away when the Giant appeared, but now they came shyly back. Spring came back too, and the Giant said, "This is your garden now children. You must come and play here when you want, and we will all share the flowers and the trees."

Then he took an axe and he knocked down the wall he had selfishly built round the garden and he threw away the notices. All day long he played with the children.

He was now the Happy Giant.

But when the children came to say goodbye,
the Giant noticed the little boy was not with
the other children.

"Where is he?" he said.

"We don't know," said the children.

"Tell him to come tomorrow," said the Giant.

"We don't know where he lives," said the children.

The Giant was sad. He loved watching his friends
playing in the garden, but he missed the little boy
he had helped into the tree.

Years went by, and the Giant became old and weak.
He sat in his armchair, smiling as he remembered how
spring had come and had made him a good giant.
He wasn't a Selfish Giant now.

It was winter in the garden, but the Giant knew that
spring would come as usual. One day he looked into the
garden and rubbed his eyes in astonishment.

In one corner of the garden, a tree had covered
itself in blossom! In winter! What could this mean?

Then he saw the little boy standing there in
the corner under the peach tree. The Giant went out
to greet him, laughing with joy. Then he stopped.
He looked at the little boy.

"Who are you?" said the Giant.

"I am the boy who played in your garden," said
the boy. "Tonight you will play in my garden.
It is called Heaven, good Giant."

When the children ran into the garden that afternoon, they found the Giant lying dead under the peach tree. It had covered him with a cloak of beautiful pink blossoms.

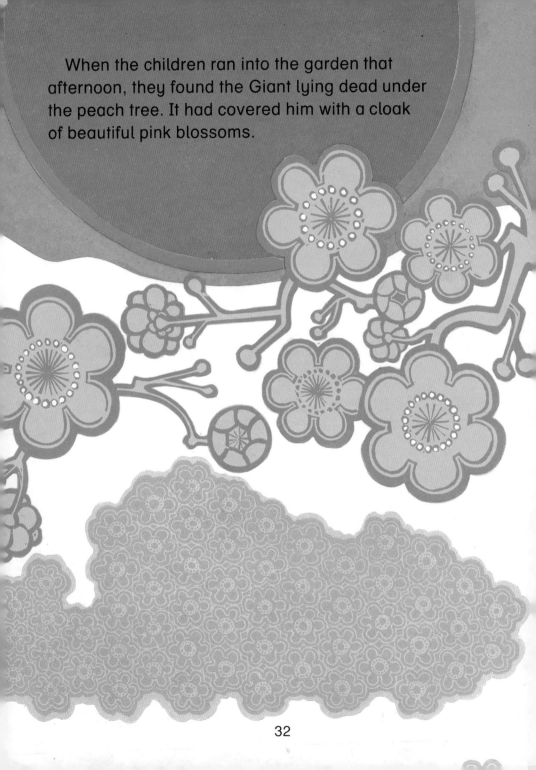